Little Sisters Are...

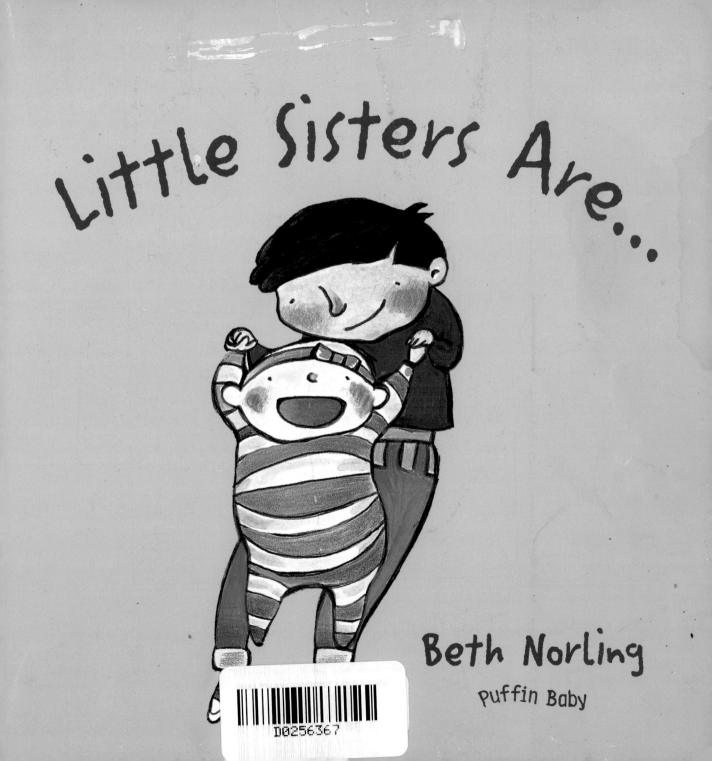

Beth Norling

Puffin Baby

Little sisters are

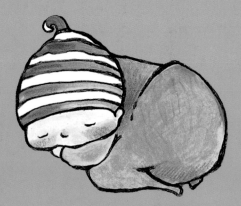

tiny...

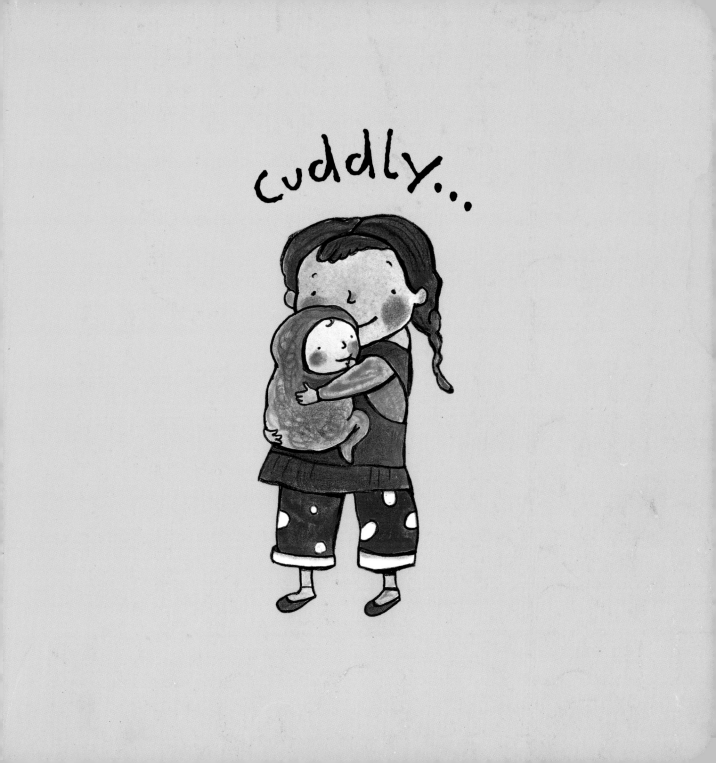

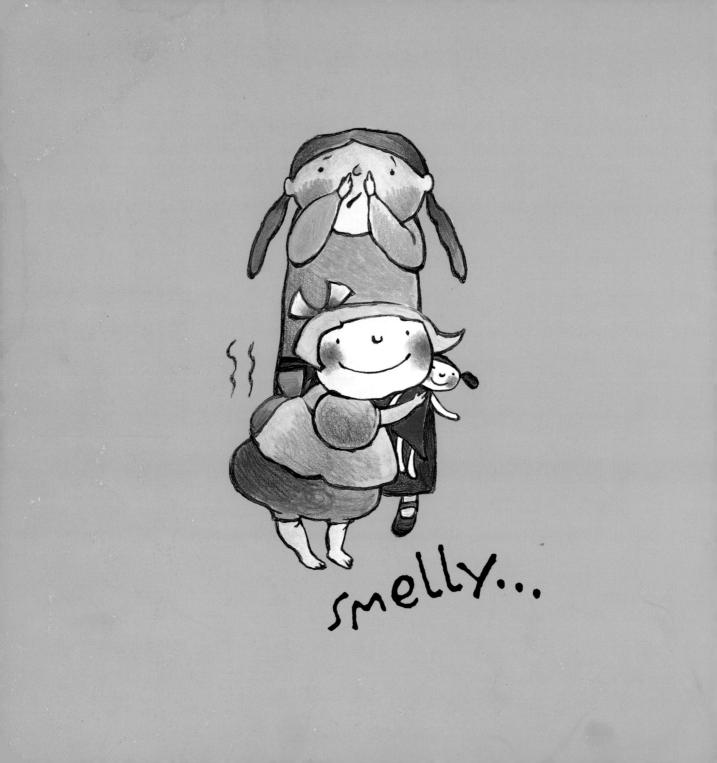

smelly...

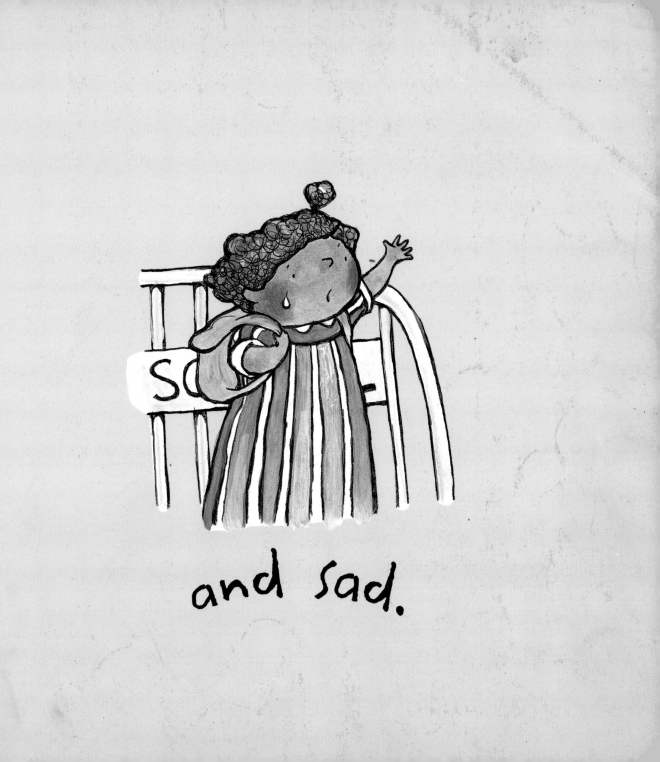

and sad.

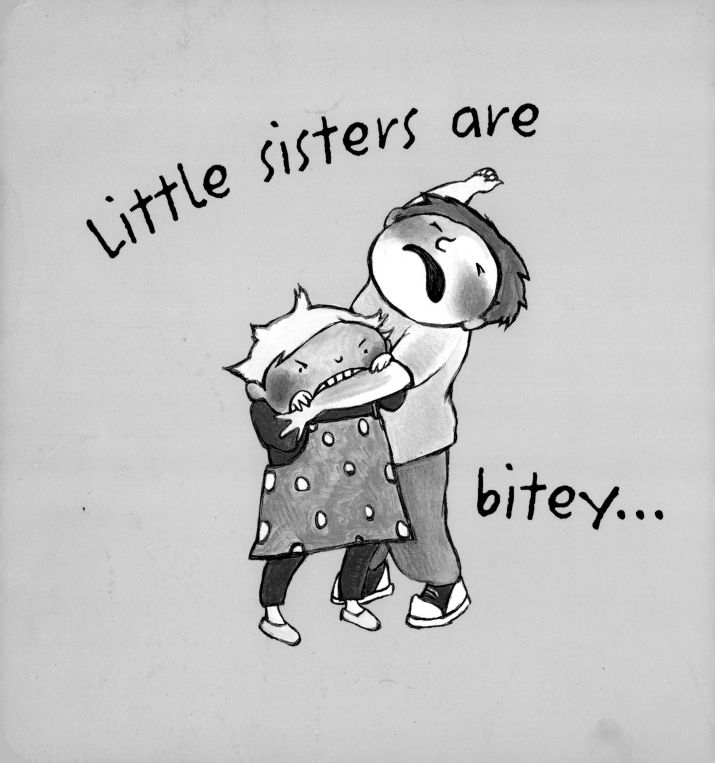

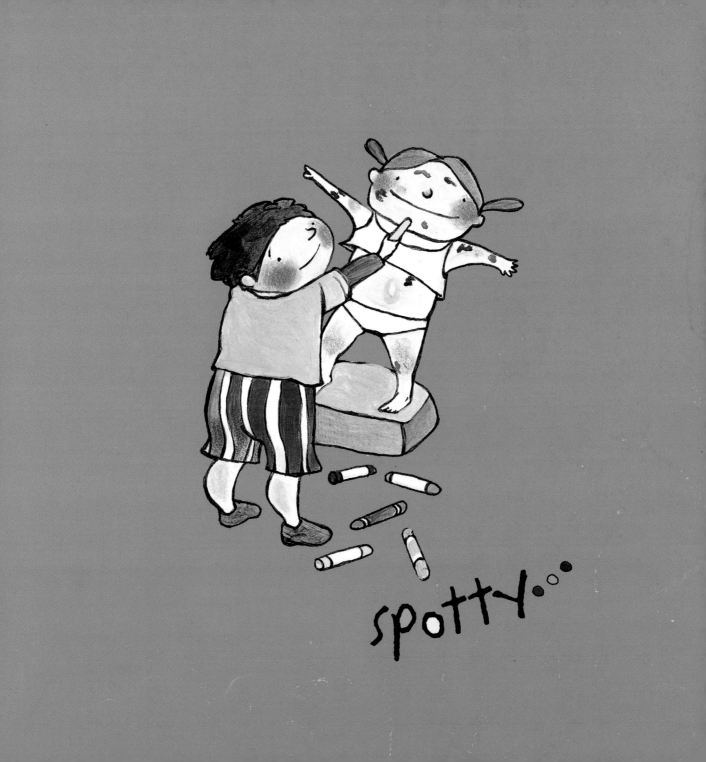

spotty

crunchy...

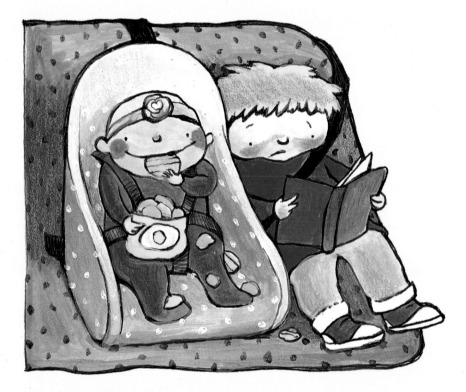

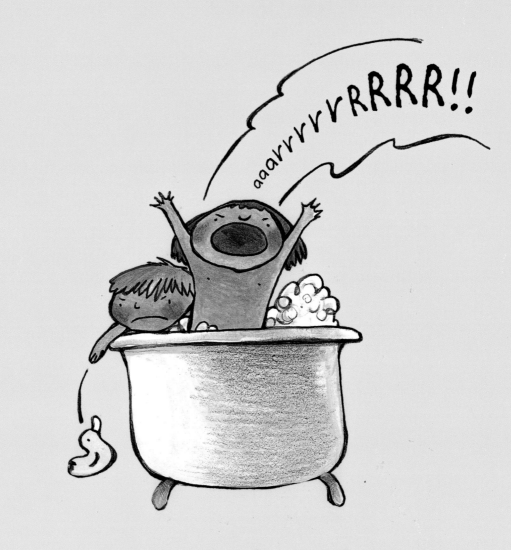

and loud.

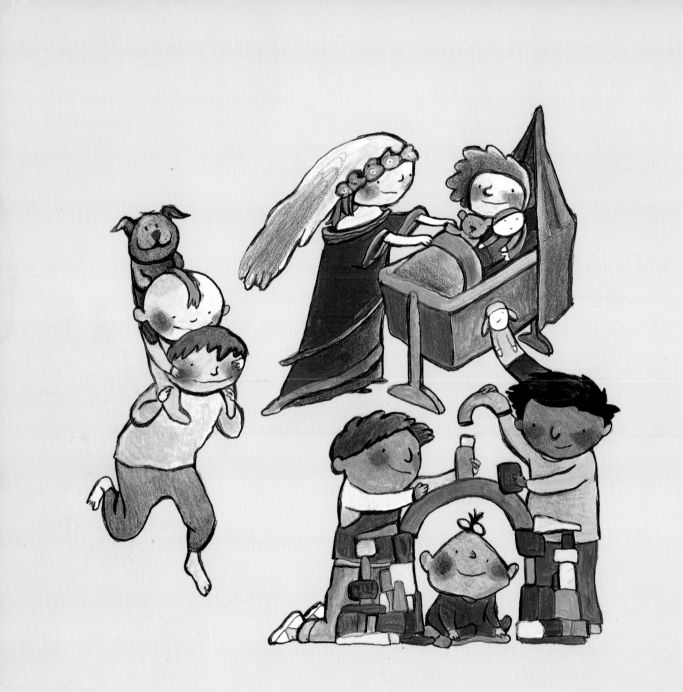

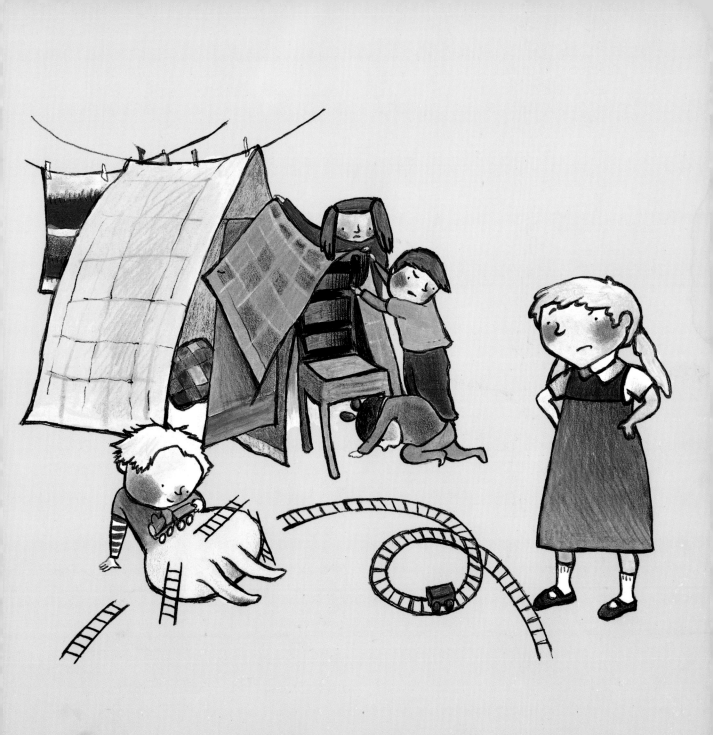

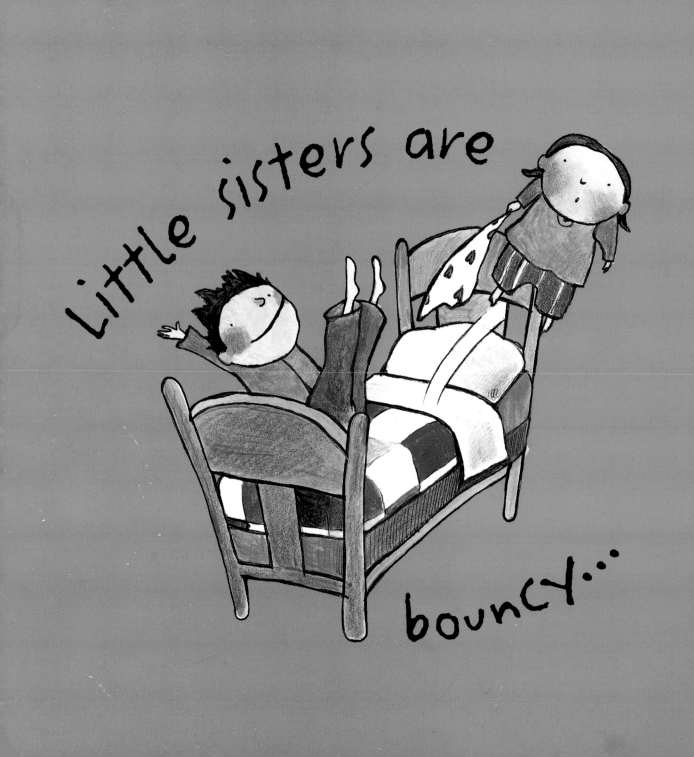

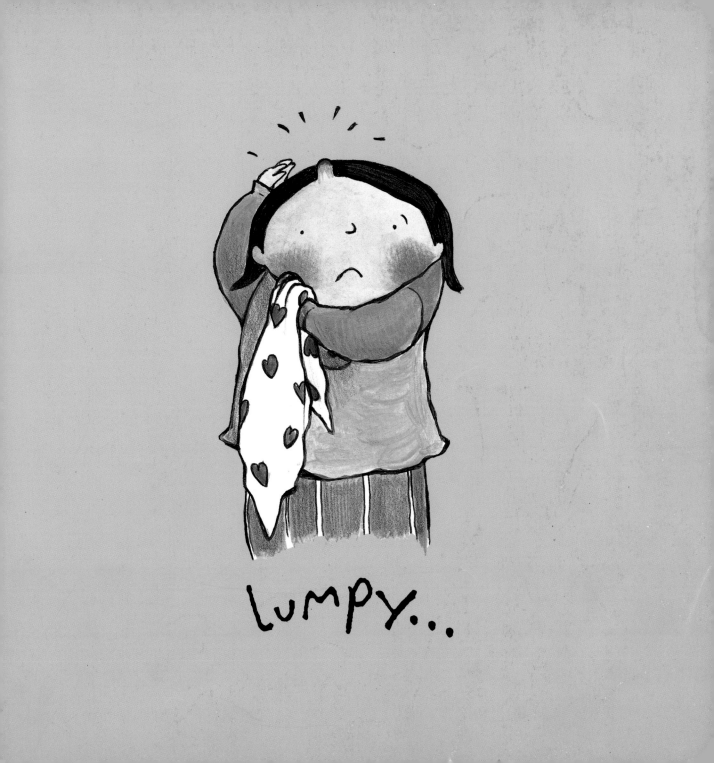

lumpy...

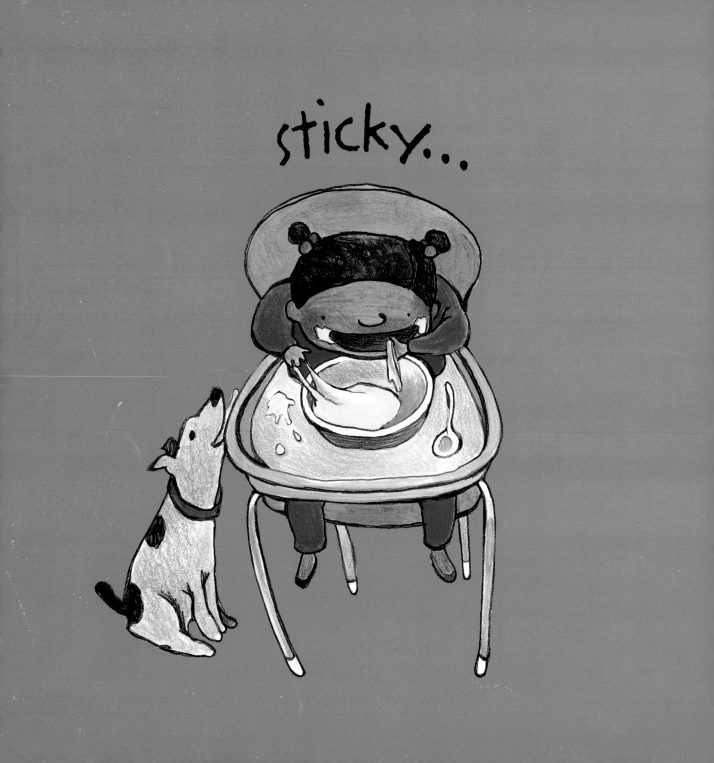

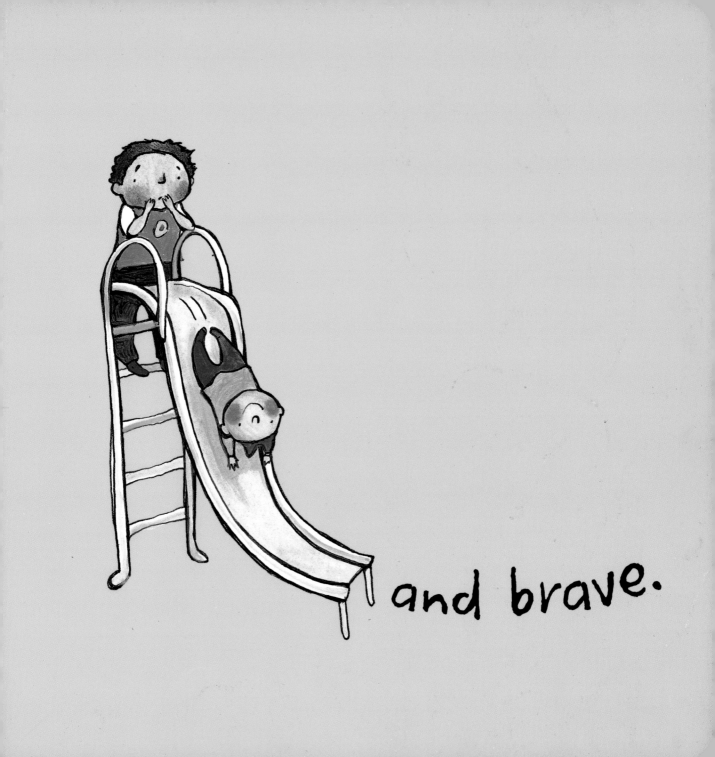

and brave.

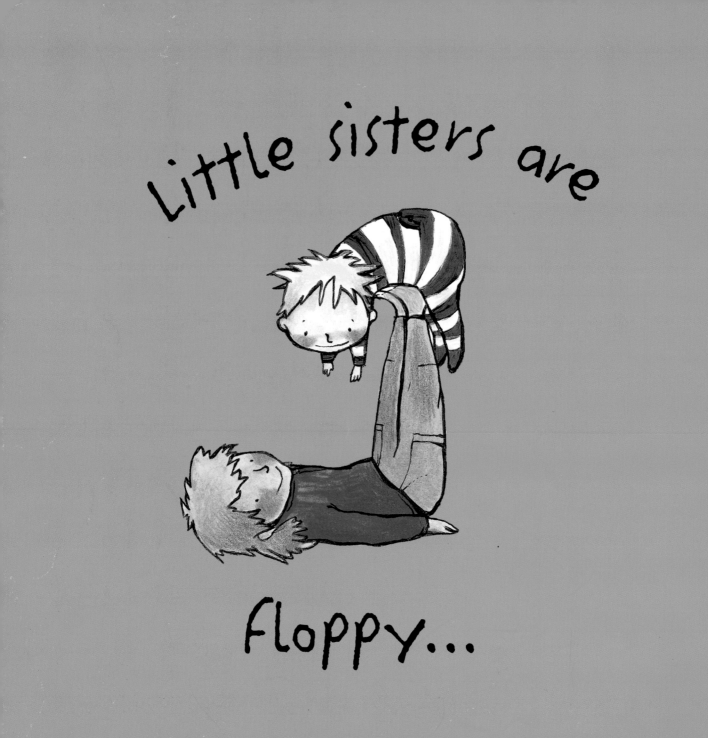

frowny...

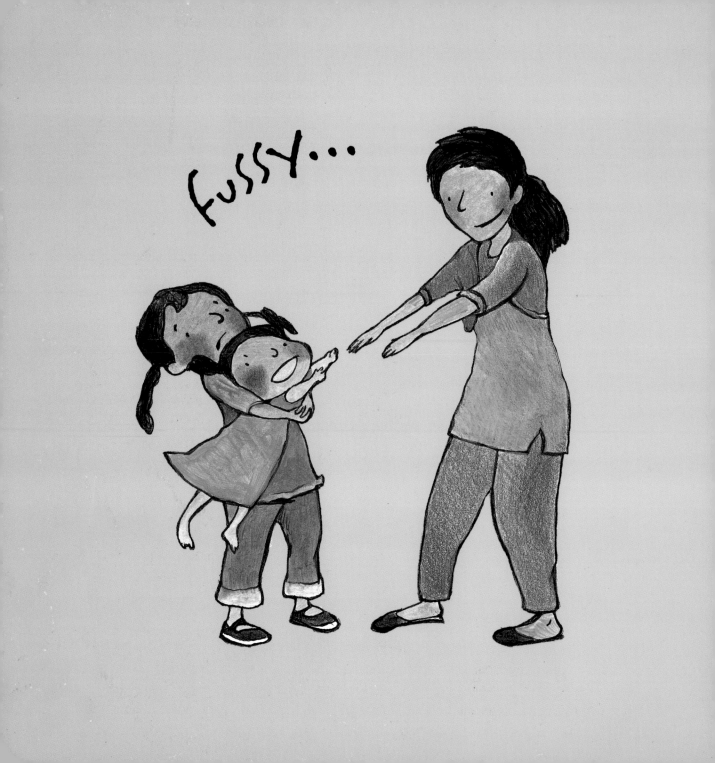

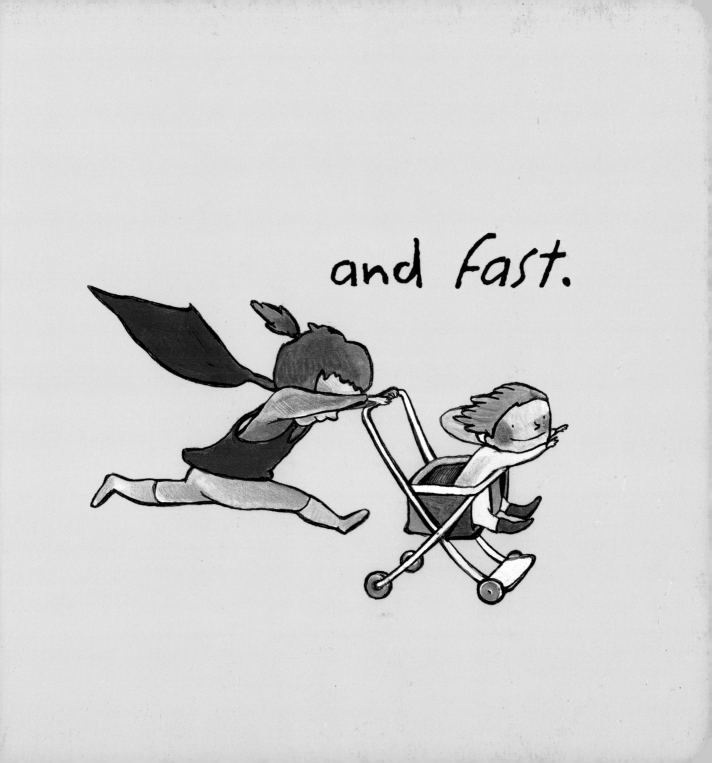

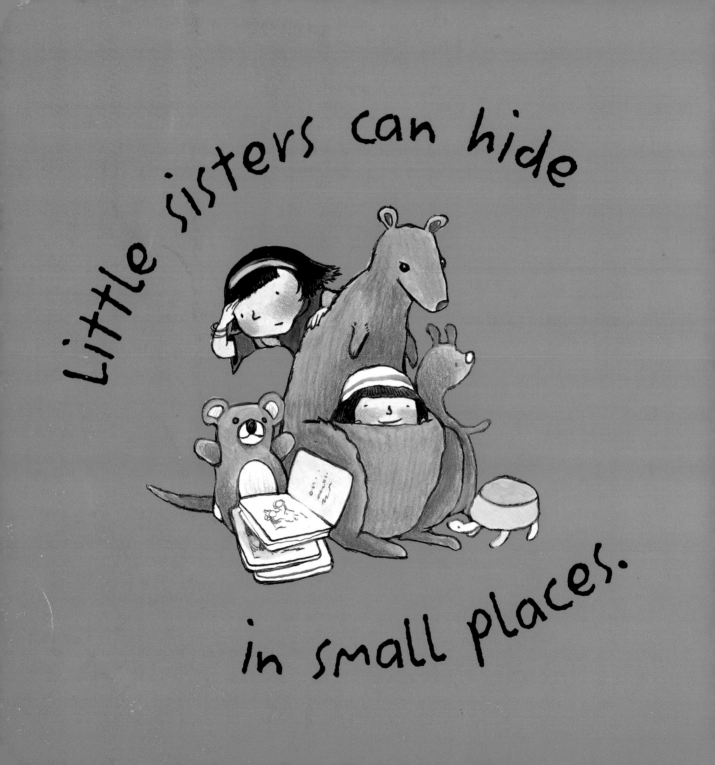

Little sisters can hide

in small places.

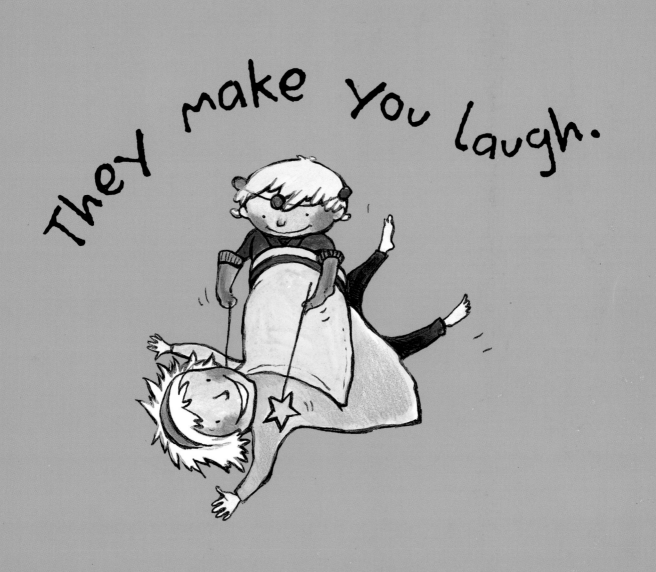

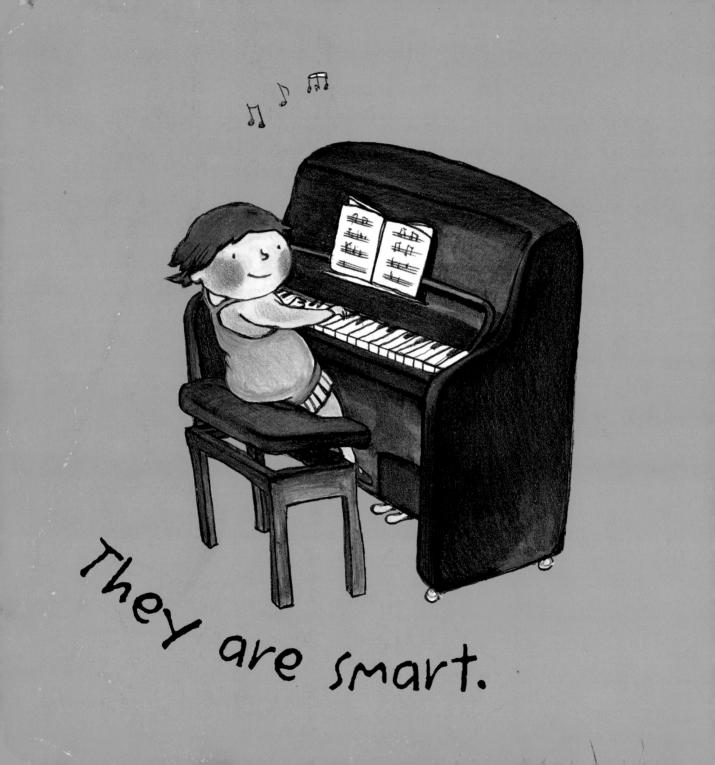

They are smart.

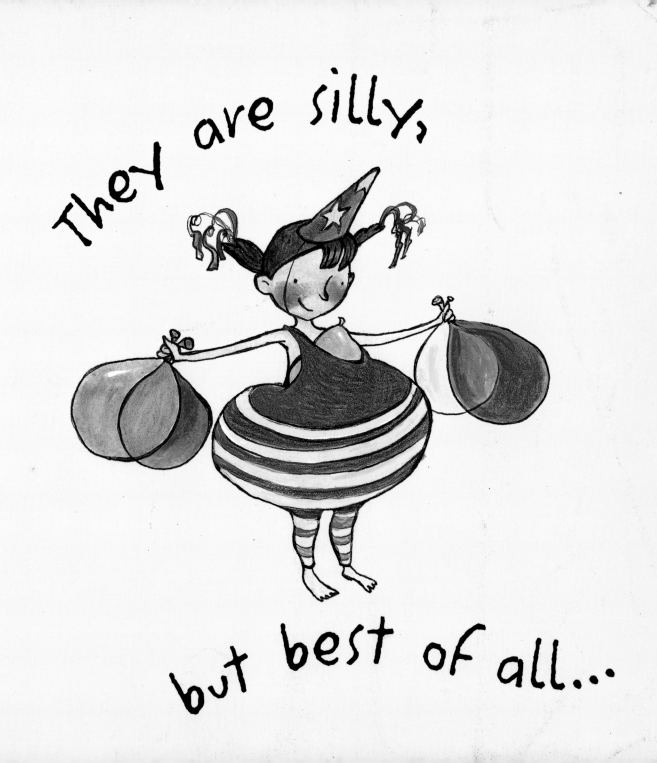

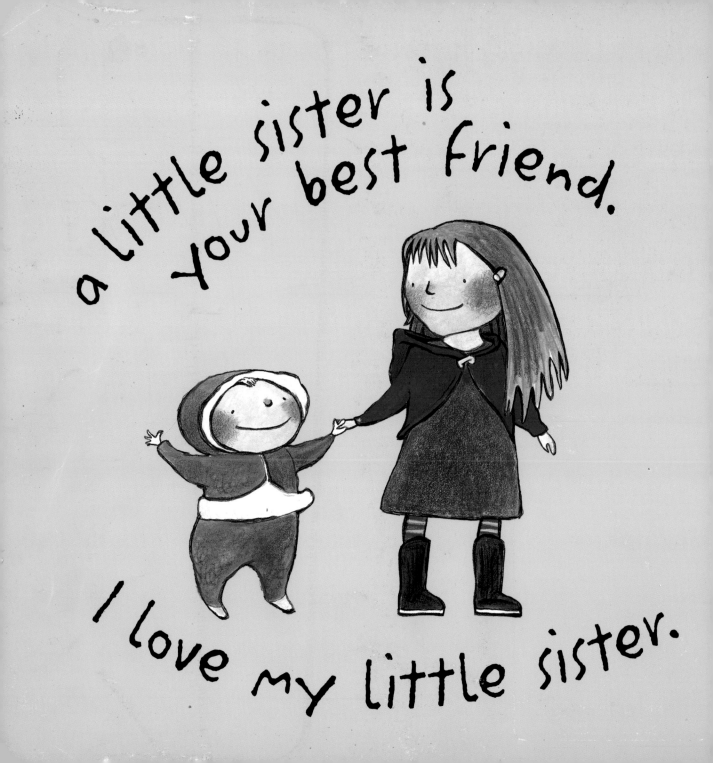